SENTENCED

By

Sheila Lee Brown

Sheila Lee Brown digitally painted the book's two illustrations ("Mosquito Attack" and "Ahna"). Prints are available for purchase at www.sheilaleebrown.com.

ISBN-978-1-946651-16-7

Published by TZ Books
www.tz-books.com

CONTENTS

The Mosquitoes Attack
Illustration by Sheila Lee Brown

Caught

"You're all dead."

Kamira froze mid-step. Beside her, Susan and Lori turned with matching expressions of confusion, their flashlights casting nervous conical beams in the night. Sister Barbara — aka *Sister Barbara the Barbarian* — stood just beyond the threshold of the cultural hall, arms crossed, mouth tight, and brow furrowed even deeper than usual.

The three girls had only just stepped outside into the thickly warm summer air and were about to head out into the night.

"Did we do something wrong?" Susan asked as she swatted at a gang of mosquitoes that had been waiting to assault the next person or persons to step outside. Kamira did the same. Lori smacked several of the bloodsuckers on her forearm and immediately whispered a quick prayer for their souls.

Sister Barbara, unbothered by the swarm, stared them down. "No. You are *actually* dead. Deceased. And you have entered the spirit realm."

Sister Barbara swirled her arms in an elaborate flourish and her unibrow rippled across her forehead. A hint of delight sparkled in her eyes as if she took pleasure at declaring the demise of teenage girls.

"Now follow me."

She turned on her heel and strode into the darkness, flashlight beam dancing across the pine needle-strewn path.

The summer camp buildings were surrounded by trees with footpaths connecting them.

Sister Barbara was heading a direction that would lead them to the activity cabins.

Kamira raised an eyebrow at Susan. Susan shrugged. Lori, already a few steps ahead, paused and motioned for them to come on.

"Hurry up!" Sister Barbara called over her shoulder without stopping.

"I don't like this," Kamira whispered, scurrying to fall in step with Susan as they caught up with Lori.

Susan muttered, "Neither do I."

"Do you think we're in trouble?" Kamira asked.

"Who knows," Susan said, frowning at Sister Barbara's back. They were lagging far enough behind the Barbarian to speak low and not be heard.

Circles of light from their flashlights bounced on the ground as they watched for roots and other trip hazards.

"How are we going to get away now?" Kamira asked.

"We'll figure it out," Susan said with determination. "Let's see what is going on first."

Lori walked in silence. Knowing her, she was probably saying a prayer for something. Maybe she was repenting for planning to sneak away from the cultural hall. Or maybe praying for the three of them since they had apparently just died. Or, perhaps she had swatted another group of mosquitoes when Kamira wasn't looking and was giving them a good send off.

Kamira glanced up ahead, noting that Sister Barbara was dressed all in white. Kamira should have noticed that right away. Nobody wore white at camp, or, if they did, it didn't stay that color very long. Day-to-day camp life was a varied experience of mud, sweat, and mystery stains.

"Do you think we're really dead?" Lori asked quietly.

Susan's hand whipped out and slapped Lori's forehead. Lori yelped and stumbled.

"No. But that mosquito is," Susan said, grinning.

Lori rubbed at the tiny splat of blood above her eyes. Kamira cracked a smile. Lori was sweet — a little too quick to believe things — but in this bizarre moment, Kamira could understand her spiritual friend asking the question. Walking through the camp at night, following a figure in white, being told they were dead...it was all sort of surreal. They had no idea what it felt or looked like to be dead. Who was to say they weren't?

"Watch this," Susan whispered, a mischievous smirk forming. She picked up her pace and closed the gap between herself and Sister Barbara.

"So, Sister Barbara," she began innocently, "how did we die? Bad sandwich meat at lunch? I *knew* that turkey smelled funny..."

Sister Barbara glared over her shoulder but kept up her pace.

"No," she said flatly.

"Then how?" Susan asked, glancing back to grin at Kamira. "We're only thirteen. Healthy. I'm sure I didn't drown in the pool or--"

"It was a plane crash!" Sister Barbara blurted without looking back.

"We were on a plane?" Susan snorted. "My parents did not authorize a plane ride--"

"A plane crashed into the camp," Sister Barbara turned enough to give Susan a dirty look as she picked up her pace. Maybe she thought walking faster would deter more questions. She should know Susan better after the last four days.

"Wow," Susan said. "It's going to be hard to get girls to come to Young Women Camp next year if there is a risk of planes crashing into the facilities." Susan looked around at the forest, and added, "Of course, if you're here with us, then you're probably dead, too, right? I guess it's not *your* problem. Why don't we see any fire or wreckage or..."

"You're dead. That's all you need to know right now," Sister Barbara snapped.

Susan smiled and was about to needle Sister Barbara anew when they saw a light through the trees up ahead.

"Is that Christine?" Susan whispered as she fell back to join her friends.

Up ahead, a circle of warm light spilled from the crafts cabin, illuminating a girl sitting quietly in a chair outside.

"I think so," Kamira said as she tilted her head to see through the trees ahead.

"Maybe she can get some aliens to help us get away," Susan said with a grin. "That would be fun."

Susan was being silly. Christine mostly kept to herself, but if you talked to her, she was probably going to go off about extraterrestrials and other weird things. She seemed like a nice person, though.

As they reached the cabin, Kamira saw a semicircle of chairs arranged in the grassy area just outside the door, eight total. Christine sat at the far end, hands in her lap, back straight.

Sheets hung over the windows inside, blocking any view of what was to happen next.

"Sit and wait your turn," Sister Barbara said, gesturing to the empty seats opposite Christine. She pointed at Susan. "Quietly. This is a time for reverence and contemplation."

With that, she turned and walked away, probably to fetch more "dead girls."

Kamira considered making a joke about spacecraft beaming them up, but Susan spoke first.

"Plane crash, huh?"

"Forest fire," Christine whispered without looking up.

Susan winced. "Oof. Sorry to hear that." She leaned in toward Christine, lowering her voice. "So... what exactly are we waiting for?"

Before Christine could respond, the cabin door opened. A man in white emerged, guiding another girl away down a side path. Kamira thought it was Brianna, though it was hard to tell in the dark. A second man stepped into the doorway and beckoned Christine inside. She stood and vanished through the door without another word.

Lori, Susan, and Kamira sat still, watching the door, for several long moments after it close, as if they were prey trying to avoid notice. Nothing else happened. As one, the three girls released a breath Kamira hadn't realized she was holding.

"This blows," Susan muttered.

"Language!" Lori said automatically.

"I mean it," Susan whispered. "Why are we just sitting here? What's stopping us from leaving?"

"Don't you get it?" Lori said. Her voice was soft but steady. "We're dead. Now we have to be judged."

Lori fidgeted with the beaded bracelet they had made the day before in the very cabin they were sitting outside of right now. Kamira instinctively touched hers, too. All three had matching bracelets around their wrists.

"Then I'm definitely going back to our cabin," Susan said, standing. Lori grabbed her arm and pulled her back down.

"The Barbarian caught us. They'll call your mom again," Lori said. "And you'll be grounded for the rest of your life. You promised you would stay out of trouble. This is our last night. We're good people. What do we have to worry about?"

Susan shifted in her chair as Lori spoke and rolled her eyes.

"How long do you think this is going to take?" she finally said.

"Someone's coming," Kamira pointed to the door and the silhouette of someone approaching.

A man in white led out another girl, someone Kamira hadn't met. He led her down a different path from the one the previous girl had taken. This girl was smiling. Behind those two was another man in white. He made eye contact with Lori and gestured for her to come into the cabin. Lori meekly stood and walked inside. The door banged shut behind her.

"This is so stupid," Susan said. "Let's get out of here before anyone else sees us."

"We can't leave Lori! And I think they will notice we are gone."

"Maybe," Susan said. "But I think we can get away with it. It looks like different people are coming and going, so who will know if we are inside or if we've been led away? And we'll grab Lori the first chance that we get."

"Wait," Kamira said. "Lori is right. You can't afford to get in more trouble and it's our last night. We should just get through this. Maybe we'll have chocolate chip cookies later, like we did on Wednesday."

"They can't make this right with cookies," Susan said as she began slapping her bare skin, taking out small platoons of mosquitoes as they landed in force. Kamira looked at her own arms and legs and began swatting guerilla style and leaving wings, legs, and bloody splat marks all over her body. It was like the creatures enjoyed the smell of repellent! "I'm going to need a blood transfusion if I have to sit out here much longer."

"But…"

Footsteps crunched nearby, cutting Kamira short.

"Now or never," Susan hissed—and then she was gone, darting into the woods beside the cabin.

Kamira hesitated, caught between instinct and reason. And then the moment was gone. From a different direction, one of the other counselors emerged from the shadows, herding three more girls toward the circle.

Kamira offered the newcomers a weak smile as they were directed to sit and wait quietly. None of the girls met her gaze. They simply took their seats and stared ahead, avoiding eye contact like they were already on trial. Kamira briefly wondered what had "killed" them— plane crash, forest fire, alien abduction—but didn't feel like asking.

She glanced toward the spot where Susan had slipped away. Gone. Or hiding well.

The death-march hum of mosquitoes hovered in stereo around the group. Kamira scratched a welt and absently toyed with the bracelet on her wrist, twisting the lettered beads until she could read the words strung between the colored ones. Their inside joke. A memento.

It had started on Tuesday morning. The three of them—Kamira, Susan, and Lori—had been asked to read the morning scripture during the flag-raising ceremony. Susan, always trying to be different, thought it would be hilarious to choose the shortest verse in the Bible. They'd stepped solemnly in front of the flagpole, and Susan had delivered her line with Shakespearean drama:

"Jeeeee-sussss wept."

Then, with over-the-top theatrical reverence, she'd closed her Bible and walked off. Lori had nervously stepped forward to clarify, "John, Chapter 11, verse 35," and Kamira had followed them both back to the group, trying not to laugh.

It had earned them a reputation. Odd. Unpredictable. Slightly irreverent. They didn't mind. It let them stay on the fringe unless camp activities dragged them into the fold. When they spotted letter beads in the craft cabin, it had only felt right to immortalize the moment in jewelry.

"JESUS WEPT"—two words separated by a single blue bead.

The verse referred to Jesus's grief over Lazarus's death—grief that came just before raising him from the dead. Now, sitting in this strange camp purgatory, Kamira stared at the bracelet and considered: Was Susan's leaving comparable to rising from the dead?

She scanned the woods again, hoping for a glimpse of her friend, but there was only darkness and mosquitoes.

The other girls remained silent, lost in whatever reverent contemplation had been demanded of them. Kamira wasn't feeling very contemplative. Mostly, she felt itchy. And annoyed. She flicked a mosquito as it landed on her leg and tried to distract herself by replaying the evening.

The day had started normally enough. Camp had its rhythms—swimming, crafts, spiritual discussions, mosquito battles—but each evening brought something different. The first night, when they'd performed skits had been a highlight. Susan had laid down with her feet in view while Lori, seated on her torso, pretended the legs were hers. Kamira played the straight character as they demonstrated increasingly bizarre stretches. It had been weird and hilarious and perfect.

Another night had been all about music—learning and performing camp songs. Other times they'd shared projects or testimonies. Tonight had been different.

When they'd first entered the cultural hall, the rows of chairs had been cleared out. Stations were set up across the room—bean bag tosses, fishing games, darts. On the stage: prizes. Real ones. Phones, tablets, headphones. The counselors had told them this was their final night at camp, and they should have fun.

So they had. They'd played everything, laughing and being silly, racking up tickets and talents. But after a while, they'd wanted to sneak back to their cabin—just the three of them—to eat snacks and talk late into the night. A final hurrah before being dumped back into real life the next morning.

They'd almost made it. Almost.

Kamira slapped at her arm and groaned. She was sure she'd have bug-bite constellations to compare with Lori later. She was mid-swat when the cabin door creaked open. Christine was being led out. She looked calm. Even smiled at Kamira in passing.

Maybe everything was okay.

Then another man in white appeared at the door and gestured for Kamira to enter. She stood and walked forward, the eyes of the newer girls tracking her with silent dread.

Behind her, she heard a faint scuffle in the brush—an annoyed sigh, maybe. She glanced back but saw nothing. The other girls didn't seem to notice.

Kamira stepped into the cabin. She may not have seen it, but she could feel the door closing behind her.

Judgment

Inside, the cabin seemed very bright. The soft ambient glow of the outside light was contrasted with an ultra white, blinding light. If they were indeed to be judged in this light, no doubt all their faults would be on full display.

The craft cabin was large, but now it was divided by hanging sheets and curtains, giving it the feel of a makeshift ER. Kamira could see several partitioned areas, each with a man seated at a desk. She did a quick scan for Lori, but the fabric was hung in a way that blocked her view of who the men were talking to. The man who had escorted her gestured toward the only empty section.

"Please sit," he said, indicating a metal-fold-up chair positioned in front of and facing the desk.

Kamira obeyed with caution, her ears straining for any sign of Lori's voice in the muffled voices nearby. She thought she heard someone crying. It was not reassuring at all.

"Do you know why you are here?" the man asked. He was sitting uncomfortably upright. Kamira shifted on the chair and cringed when it made an awkward sound rubbing on the plank flooring. She sat up straighter and attempted to feel more in control.

"I'm... dead?" she offered. "A plane crashed into the camp."

Kamira had hoped he would laugh at the absurdity of what Sister Barbara had told them, but he nodded solemnly.

"And do you understand where you are now?"

"Well…," Kamira began. She thought about what Lori had said about being judged, but she didn't want to say that and sound stupid. She also thought about saying it was the craft cabin, but that sounded too snarky and Susan-ish. She would likely get in trouble. She settled on, "Not really."

The man leaned forward slightly. "How long have you been a member of the Church?"

"All my life."

"Good," he said, nodding again. "So you know about Judgment. And the Three Kingdoms?"

Kamira nodded. Of course she knew. They learned all that from an early age. The afterlife of the Latter-Day Saints church was one of the major differences between them and typical Christian churches.

Instead of heaven and hell, there were three kingdoms, round like planets, where a spirit would be sent after death: the Telestial, the Terrestrial, or the Celestial, with the Telestial being the lowest and the Celestial being the highest that a person could attain. The other option was Outer Darkness, which sounded really scary, but was pretty hard to get into unless you were a particularly horrible person.

"Good," the man said again. "Let's begin, then. How many tickets do you have?"

Kamira's eyes widened at the question. While playing the games in the cultural hall, tickets or talents were given, depending on the game. Kamira reached into her pocket and slowly pulled out a handful of slightly crumpled tickets. The man looked them over and nodded.

"How many talents do you have?"

Kamira went to reach into her pocket and hesitated, her face growing hot. She remembered one of the other girls coming up to them before they left.

"Hey, do you have some talents?" the girl asked.

"Yeah," Lori said and Kamira had nodded yes.

"Maybe," Susan replied. She was watching the girl with narrowed eyes. Kamira thought the girl's name was Jeri or something like that. Jeri was one of the junior counselors and had never really talked to any of them before. That should have been the first red flag.

"Can I have them?" Jeri asked.

Kamira, Lori, and Susan hesitated, looking to one another for a response.

"Uh...," Lori began.

"Why do you want them?" Susan asked.

"Oh, yeah," Jeri said. "I'm still hungry and need them to get food."

"We need talents to get dinner?" Kamira asked.

"No, not to get dinner," Jeri said. "Just if you want seconds. And I'm really hungry." She rubbed her stomach. Something about it had felt off - like Jeri had been putting on a bit of a show. Red flag #2.

"Sorry," Susan said, one eyebrow raised. "Maybe someone else can help."

"Susan!" Lori had cut in. "Of course we'll give her our talents. We can always get more if we want them."

Susan frowned. Kamira shrugged. They all dug out their talents and handed them over to Jeri. She smiled and walked away, moving towards another girl who had just finished playing a game. Kamira thought she overheard her asking for more talents and wondered how many a person needed to get more food when Susan's voice distracted her, saying that it looked like a good time to head out.

Now she was facing down this strange man who was asking for the talents she had given away. It was obvious where this conversation was going. Tickets versus talents. She remembered which games gave the tickets and which gave the talents. All the church games gave talents and there were no prizes for talents on the stage. All the prizes were ticket-based.

"I… don't have any," she admitted with a gulp. She bit the edge of her bottom lip as her mind processed it all. They had been duped. And by someone Kamira felt they should have been able to trust.

The man's expression shifted — not angry, but disappointed. That was worse.

"I gave them away," she said quickly. Surely there was an exception if you were tricked! "To a girl who said she needed them for food."

"How many did you have?" the man asked. He still looked disappointed, but he seemed to understand that some people had figured out the set-up and had cheated.

"I don't know. I didn't count."

The man sighed. Not meanly. Just heavily.

"In that case," he said, "I will have to sentence you to the Telestial Kingdom. As you know--the lowest."

Kamira bit her lip again, this time to keep herself from swearing. That was definitely Susan rubbing off on her. She wanted to protest, to argue that it wasn't fair. But the man's face was unreadable. No room for negotiation.

"Wait here while I find someone to escort you," he said.

Kamira sat in silence, burning with shame and fury. How could Jeri have done that! Didn't she have any conscience?

Eventually, the man returned with another man dressed in white.

"Time to go," the new man said.

Kamira followed, her thoughts spinning.

Outside the cabin, only two of the girls she'd left behind were still waiting. Two new ones sat beside them, pale and quiet. She hadn't been able to see them coming in and out.

The new man in white led her into the woods. No words. No names. Maybe names didn't matter in purgatory.

Kamira's annoyance churned with each step. Jeri had played them — and the system. How many others had fallen for it?

As the path narrowed and the trees thickened, Kamira's night vision adjusted. She could make out pine needles scattered like brittle confetti. A faint rustle came from the trees to her right.

Movement.

Kamira shifted her gaze without turning her head. A shadow slipped from one trunk to another.

And then — a face. Susan.

Kamira's heart lifted. Of course her trusty friend had followed.

She kept walking, stealing glances toward the trees. Susan darted between shadows like a mischievous sprite. Kamira decided then and there — if she was going to be stuck in the Telestial Kingdom, she was going to make the best of it.

She started to perform.

First, a goofy walk — arms swinging wide. Then a little spin. A shuffle. A twirl that ended in a hard landing.

The man turned.

"Sorry," Kamira said quickly. "Thought I saw something move. I didn't want to step on it. I, uh... *really* love living things."

The man tilted his head slightly. "We're almost there."

He resumed walking. Kamira sneaked another glance. Susan was barely holding in laughter.

Kamira grinned.

She was already planning her escape when a cabin appeared up ahead. Dark. Silent. The kind of quiet that drags out in horror movie before a big jump scare. Kamira glanced at the woods, looking for another sign of Susan. She didn't see one.

The man opened the door and motioned for her to enter. Kamira stepped inside.

Before she could speak, the screen door snapped shut behind her with a final, springy *thud*.

Inside was a single room, like all the other cabins they slept in, with cots pushed up against the walls. This cabin was slightly larger than the 4-cot cabins they slept in, though. Not only were there no cabin lights on, it was hot. A small heater was on in the middle of the cabin, its hot coils highlighting a myriad of young girls' faces reflected in its red-orange glow.

Doing Time

"Sit down!"

The voice snapped Kamira to attention. She flinched and dropped onto the nearest cot — and instantly regretted it. A sharp spring jabbed her thigh through the thin mattress covering.

"Not there! On the floor!"

Kamira scooted off the cot and dropped cross-legged onto the floor, her pulse pounding in her ears. She grimaced in pain as her butt slammed down on the hard surface, but she stayed quiet. This scenario was so far from anything she would have imagined at camp, that she wasn't sure what to do. She watched and waited.

The cabin was now eerily silent. Perhaps that had been the worst of it?

Kamira glanced around the room, only moving her eyes, assessing how everyone else was handling the situation. They all looked as uncomfortable and uncertain as Kamira felt.

The air in the cabin was stifling. The acrid scent of sweat hung in the air, dense and sour. A dozen or so girls sat around on the floor, their faces glistening and flushed. She noticed the occasional shift in discomfort, but there was no indication that anyone was prepared to say or do anything other than sit and sweat.

Then Kamira saw a familiar silhouette, a face bowed in contemplation: Lori. At least they were together. Kamira allowed herself to relax as much as she was able. The one positive thing was that they were no longer outside where the mosquitoes could attack. Kamira heard a familiar hum in her ear as if to remind her who was calling the shots.

Kamira sighed to herself and tugged lightly at her t-shirt neck, trying to create airflow between her skin and the fabric without attracting any more screams. It didn't help.

It was uncomfortably warm. The summer weather was already hot even in the night and the fact that they were running a heater seemed like overkill. It was almost as if they were trying to make the Telestial kingdom feel like Hell (which Kamira always told her Baptist classmates that she didn't believe in).

She wished Susan was there. She would have surely livened things up. Kamira imagined Susan walking in, assessing the situation, and saying something like, *"Wow. This seems like some sort of human rights violation."*

And then it would be on between her and the yelling lady.

Kamira grinned at the thought, but stopped abruptly, suddenly hyperaware of the woman, the yelling lady, at the center of the room:

Sister Thompson. She was seated near the heater, arms folded, her face set in a scowl that dared anyone to test her.

Sister Thompson had volunteered to help with camp that week — one of the "cool moms," allegedly. Not tonight. She looked really annoyed. She probably wasn't enjoying having to sit in the cabin with them. And it wouldn't be getting any better. Nobody's deodorant was holding up to the abnormal rise in temperature.

The screen door creaked open, and another girl stumbled in. Mandy. Kamira recognized her from their CPR class. Mandy froze, blinking at the red-lit gloom.

"Sit down!"

Mandy dropped to the floor instantly, avoiding the second shriek that Kamira had received.

Then it was back to silence and literal stewing. Looking around the cabin, a revolt didn't seem likely, even though it was one adult against a dozen or more teens. They all seemed willing to wait it out, much like Kamira had been when waiting outside the craft cabin. *If only she had listened to Susan!* But then Lori would be here alone.

Kamira wondered if they were going to be expected to stay there all night. She knew it had to be after 8 PM already. She wished they had gotten dinner. One, she wouldn't be as hungry as she was and, two, they would've known that Jeri was lying to them about getting seconds.

Kamira thought of the snacks waiting in their cabin — chips, candy, chocolate snack cakes. Their plan had been to sneak away and eat it all while talking late into the night. A perfect send-off. They'd been so close. Her stomach growled loudly.

"Quiet!" Sister Thompson yelled.

Kamira's stomach obeyed.

Trying to take her mind off her hunger, Kamira wondered if Susan was still outside and how long she might wait around before going back to the cabin. A thump on a nearby shutter made everyone in the cabin jump.

Kamira held her breath. Then came more thumps. Laughter. Voices.

"You're all loooooooooosers!"

A chorus of teen girls outside, shouting, taunting, and pounding on the shutters.

"The Telestial Kingdom sucks!"

"We were in the Celestial Kingdom! You're not as good as us!"

"We had air conditioning. Is it hot enough in there for you?"

"Sorry you don't have cookies and milk like we did. You should have been better."

"I bet you wish you had cookies! Losers!"

"Loooooooooosers! Loooosers! Looosers!"

Soon, that's all they were chanting.

"Losers! Losers! Losers!"

The chanting echoed around the cabin, ridiculous and surreal. Kamira almost laughed — except the part about the cookies *did* sting.

After a couple more rounds of beating the outside of the shutters and shouting "Losers!", the noise stopped, and Kamira could hear laughter and giggles moving away.

Silence reclaimed the room.

Kamira was worried her stomach would growl at the thought of cookies, but she was saved from getting yelled at again by another round of cabin thumpers. More young women voices filled the night.

"Ew! I bet it smells funky in there!"

"At least we had a fan in the Terrestrial Kingdom."

"How are you dumb enough to end up in the Telestial Kingdom? Didn't you even *try*?"

"We're awesome and you suck!"

Kamira rolled her eyes. This was starting to feel like some kind of bad sleepaway camp-themed reality show.

"Ow!"

The thumping stopped as someone said, "I just got hit with a pinecone."

"You okay? I know first aid," another voice said, sounding hopeful.

"Back off. I'm fine. It just hit me in the face."

A moment of silence. Kamira smirked. That had to be Susan. Her aim was legendary.

"It probably fell. Let's go."

There were a couple of half-hearted thumps on the cabin and they headed away. From a distance, Kamira heard the fading words, "You all suuuuuuuuuck!"

Kamira let herself slump, just a little.

She was surprised when Sister Thompson's voice filled the room again, but this time soft.

"I hope you all learned something tonight," Sister Thompson said. "We're going to be leaving here soon, but I want you all to really think about what happened and the choices that you made that brought you here. Was this fun? Do you really want to end up in the Telestial Kingdom when you die?"

Kamira held her breath. She couldn't tell if she was supposed to feel guilt, shame, regret — or all of it.

"We're going to join the other girls in the amphitheater," Sister Thompson said as she switched off the heater and stood. "Everyone out."

A slight breeze meandered its way through the sultry night air, turning the yuckiness of being overly sweaty into a blessing of body temp regulation. Kamira inhaled and exhaled deeply as the girls filed out, glad that part was over. She lingered near the back until Lori appeared beside her. They walked together in silence.

Susan popped out from the shadows and joined them.

"You had the right idea," Kamira whispered.

Susan shrugged. "We're back together. On to the next thing. Where are we headed?"

"To the amphitheater," Lori said.

"I'd say let's make a break for it," Susan muttered, "but I'm pretty sure The Barbarian spotted me. Don't look — she's watching us."

Kamira sighed. "I'm starving."

"This can't go on much longer," Susan said as she gauged the weariness of the Telestial girls ahead of them. "We have to wake up early, right?"

They walked on silently but with purpose, as if arriving faster would make the whole thing end sooner.

Around them, the other girls had begun to recover and were chatting like nothing had happened. That didn't sit right with Kamira. Something had.

And now they had to see it to the end.

Observation

The three girls emerged from the woods into a clearing at the top of a hill. Below, the amphitheater lay just as it had on the first day of camp: wooden benches built into the slope, facing a small, raised stage.

"Which kingdom were you in?" a sister asked.

"Telestial," Lori said softly. Kamira nodded beside her.

"I'm with them," Susan added.

The sister directed them to the back row.

Kamira sat, the rough wood pressing against her thighs. Lori and Susan flanked her. She scanned the crowd — and then spotted Jeri. Front and center in the Celestial Kingdom group, laughing and glowing as if she'd won the lottery.

Kamira nudged her friends.

"Cheater," Lori whispered.

"Language!" Susan shot back with a grin.

Lori stuck out her tongue. Susan ignored it.

"It was the talents, right? They used those to place you?" Susan asked, and Kamira and Lori nodded. "Guess that's how you win at life," Susan said with a shrug. "Take advantage of people. And you even get to rub it in that you won."

Kamira didn't answer. Her hands twisted in her lap.

On stage, Sister Thompson stood with several counselors. The murmurs died down as she began to speak.

"As young women, you have many opportunities ahead of you. The choices you make now — even as teenagers — can shape your entire future."

Kamira crossed her arms, feeling like they were being set up again.

"We always plan a special event for the final night of camp, something that helps impress upon you the importance of your choices. Will you choose worldly treasure... or heavenly treasure?"

She paused for several moments, letting her words hang.

"We're here to guide you. Every woman on this stage has stood where you are. We've made mistakes, and we've learned. The best advice we can give you? Let your faith be your compass. Ask yourself, 'Is this in line with what I believe? Would God want me to do this?' Let your actions reflect your values."

Kamira stared at her feet, unsure what to feel—inspired or manipulated.

Sister Thompson continued, her voice gentle. "Choose friends who share your values. Don't compromise your standards to fit in. You are a child of God. Worthy of love and respect."

Kamira glanced sideways at Susan, then Lori. That part about friends felt true, at least.

"And finally: challenge yourself. Develop your talents. God gave you those gifts for a reason."

Sister Thompson let her words linger before concluding, "I bear my testimony that this church is true, and I am grateful for each of you. I pray you keep God at the center of your lives and live true to your convictions. I say these things in the name of Jesus Christ. Amen."

The chorus of "amen" followed — even from Susan, as if by reflex.

Sister Barbara took the mic with her signature flourish. "We'll now pass the microphones. If anyone would like to share a testimony or a reflection about this week, this is your opportunity."

Kamira spotted the mic moving down a few rows.

"I'd like to bear my testimony..." a girl began, voice trembling with sincerity.

Kamira tuned out. Her mind drifted through the events of the past week.

They had arrived on Monday. The week had been filled with swimming, wilderness skills, skits, laughter — and of course, mosquitoes. Kamira could think of a dozen moments that made her smile.

But now, other memories rose to the surface.

Like the first day — when they'd stood in this very amphitheater, each forced to take a "walking stick" and repeat the words, "If you can't do this, then you're dumb, dumb, dumb." The trick was you had to clear your throat before beginning, then tap the stick three times as you said it. Get it wrong, and you had to do it again — over and over. Kamira had barely passed by copying the girl before her exactly.

Or the mess hall rule: elbows on the table meant you had to stand and do something embarrassing. Sing. Dance. Moo like a cow. It was all "in good fun," unless you were the one singled out.

And then there was Christine's ET plushie — stolen just that morning. Sister Barbara had announced it over lunch. Half the room had laughed. The other half had smirked.

Kamira clenched her hands. These weren't examples of love or respect. These were games of humiliation. Were these really the values they wanted to instill during camp?

Why would girls who had earned a place in the higher kingdoms feel like they had to make fun of the ones who didn't? Shouldn't they be compassionate? Shouldn't compassion be a requisite for being in a higher realm?

"You ready to go yet?" Susan whispered, breaking through Kamira's thought spiral of injustice. Lori surprisingly nodded yes.

Kamira hesitated. She did want to leave, but her thoughts had gotten her worked up. Her eyes drifted to the mic — now only a few people away. Her heart thudded.

She imagined standing up. Her voice cutting through the hush:

"I'd like to bear my testimony. I don't know what is true anymore. Your actions should match your words and I've looked up to you all but tonight showed me that your true colors are cheating, judging, and putting other people down. Your lesson sucked!"

In her mind, Susan stood and clapped. Lori looked mortified. The mic was snatched from her hands. Or maybe, just maybe, the girls would listen and she and her friends would rise on a tide of awakened, angry Telestialites to be ushered out into the night where they would scurry away to . . . what?

What would be the point?

Kamira glanced over at the microphone. The girl next to Susan took it and Susan held out her hand to take it and then it would pass to Kamira.

Kamira's pulse surged. Did she *want* to speak? Was she really about to embarrass herself, her friends, and her family? She braced herself to take the microphone.

Instead, the girl next to Susan stood and began bearing her testimony. It gave Kamira a moment to breathe and think things through. She couldn't pinpoint why she was suddenly so angry about things and not understanding it made her doubt herself. The testimony turned out to be super short. A murmur of "amen" from the group signaled the girl was already done. The microphone moved through Susan and into Kamira's hand. Kamira gripped it tight, noting Susan's raised eyebrows when she didn't pass it on.

Another girl was speaking, though, through one of the other microphones making the rounds. Kamira looked up.

It was Jeri — full of tears and trembling voice, thanking God and her camp friends. The counselors beamed. The girls nodded like an angel had sprung forth in their midst.

Kamira's grip on the mic tightened even more.

She glanced over at Lori. Lori looked at Kamira, then down at the microphone, and then back at Kamira.

Lori shrugged, as if to let Kamira know she should do what she wanted. It was an odd sensation, a feeling of elation that Kamira was about to be heard in a way that she hadn't expressed herself before. She heard the familiar words that indicated a testimony was coming to a close.

"I say these things in the name of Jesus Christ..."

As Kamira prepared herself to stand up, she caught the swinging movement of a CTR ring on a string hanging around the neck of the girl sitting next to Lori as she leaned forward to get a better look at Jeri.

CTR stood for "Choose the Right." They had earned those rings as children in Primary, a time when things seemed less complicated. The words struck something within Kamira, though. Everything she was getting ready to say felt stuck in her throat.

With a quick gulp, she handed off the microphone to Lori, and it went on its way down the row. Lori looked a question at Kamira and Kamira felt Susan's poke on her other side. She knew they would want to talk about this later.

Jeri's words faded. The rest of the testimonies blurred together.

Kamira was ready to call it a night. Kamira wasn't sure what she would say to Susan and Lori... She wasn't sure she could explain why she didn't stand up.

It wasn't fear (well, maybe a little). At that last moment, it just didn't feel right to speak out in anger.

As soon as the testimonies ended and the girls were dismissed, Kamira, Susan, and Lori bolted down the path towards their cabin.

"I'm glad that's over," Susan said as they walked. "I mostly understand what happened, but details would be great."

"I wish you had been in there," Kamira said. "Well, not that I wish you were in the Telestial Kingdom, but if you had seen what it was like ... hey, did you throw that pinecone at the Terrestrial girls?"

Susan answered with a chuckle. Kamira laughed, and for the first time since the night went sideways, she felt a sense of relief.

Kamira mentioned how Sister Thompson was yelling at people and how hot it was. Lori was quiet. When they were about halfway down the path to their cabin, Lori tugged on Kamira's shirt sleeve and pointed toward the woods.

"Is that Jeri?"

Sure enough, Jeri and another girl were veering off-trail, something cradled in Jeri's arms.

"Let's follow them," Kamira said.

"I just want to go to bed," Lori groaned, finally finding her voice again.

"But what if she's up to something?" Kamira said. "Maybe we can stop it."

That got Lori's attention. Susan was already creeping forward like a spy.

"Follow me. I'll show you my sneaking skills," she whispered with a grin.

Kamira looked around. Most cabins had their lights on. No one seemed to be watching. She followed Susan into the woods, with Lori reluctantly behind.

Leaves crunched. Twigs snapped. Jeri didn't look back once.

The girls followed until Jeri stopped at a cabin and knocked. Christine opened the door — her face lit up.

Kamira leaned forward. Jeri handed her the ET plushie.

"She's returning it?" Susan whispered. "Did she *take* it in the first place?"

"We need to get closer," Kamira said.

They crept forward, hiding behind a cluster of trees.

Susan tiptoed to the window, listened, and returned.

"They're just talking. Laughing. Jeri said Cabin 10 took the plushie and she got it back."

"That's weird," Kamira said, furrowing her brow. "Is she playing a trick on Christine?"

"She sounded genuine," Susan said, looking at Kamira and Lori, her head tilted. "We could all tell she was lying about something in the cultural hall, right?"

Kamira frowned. She did know intuitively that something wasn't right when Jeri asked for the talents, but she didn't want to believe that Jeri had now done something nice for Christine. It didn't line up with her expectations.

"Guess we can finally go to our cabin now?" Lori asked.

"Yeah, let's call it a night," Kamira said.

Back at their cabin, Susan collapsed onto her cot.

"At last," she said, flopping back. Then she sprang up. "Time for snacks?"

Kamira chuckled. "Nothing fazes you, does it?"

"Well, I didn't have to sit in a hot cabin with people mocking me," Susan said. "Are you two okay?"

"I guess," Kamira said. She still felt a twinge of injustice, but it seemed a moot point. "The whole thing was so stupid."

Lori shrugged.

"I never thought I would end up in the Telestial Kingdom," she said.

"And you wouldn't," Susan said. "You're the nicest person I know. And the churchiest. These people are the only ones who would put you there. It's ridiculous. Did you even tell them that Jeri cheated?"

"Doesn't matter," Lori said. "What if I am a nice person? What does it matter if I let someone take advantage of me and trick me out of earning my place in a higher kingdom?"

"How could we have known?" Kamira said, feeling the truth and sting of her friend's words. "We thought we were being nice. Isn't it on Jeri to pay for tricking people?"

"What if Jeri was part of the test? Maybe they had her go around to see if people would give up their talents?" Lori said. "And we fell for it."

"Whoa," Susan said. "This is getting way too serious for our last night."

"It *is* serious," Lori said. "Sister Thompson was right. This should be a wake-up call."

"A wake-up call to *what*?" Kamira asked gently.

No one had an answer.

Crickets filled the silence.

"Maybe we should pray about it," Lori suggested.

"Pray?" Susan said. "What good will that do?"

"It couldn't hurt," Kamira said.

Lori's eyes lit up. "This is just like Joseph Smith praying for answers. We're in the perfect place--the woods." Lori looked towards the cabin door.

"Maybe we should go outside..."

"I'm not going outside this cabin," Susan said. "I have to draw the line there. I have no interest in being a blood sacrifice to mosquitoes."

"That's fair," Lori replied, tapping her chin in thought. "We can do it here. Let's kneel together by my cot." Lori directed her friends beside her so they would face the same way.

Susan and Kamira knelt beside Lori.

"You lead," Kamira whispered to Lori.

They bowed their heads.

And then, before Lori even spoke... something happened.

Kamira felt a warm sensation spreading from her lower stomach throughout her body. Her eyes were still partially open and movement in the center of the cabin caught her attention.

It appeared to be an orb of light that was growing larger and larger. She heard a gasp from Lori, and Susan grabbed her arm.

The light took on a more human shape as they watched it in wide-eyed, mouth-gaping astonishment.

Covenant

"Are you two seeing a bird person?" Susan

whispered, eyes wide.

Kamira nodded, speechless. Lori simply stared, mesmerized.

The being shimmered in a soothing shade of turquoise. Its eyes were larger than human and a luminous brown. Its face lacked a nose—just two nostril slits—and the chin tapered into a soft point. From its forehead swept a crown of elegant feathers, like a headdress that drifted down its back. It wore a layered robe that hugged its arms and flared toward the floor. Kamira glimpsed thick, scaled toes — two on each foot, birdlike and blue.

Its hands were tucked into opposite sleeves. It radiated stillness.

"I am Ahna," the being said, bowing slightly. Its voice was feminine, with a soft musical trill that lingered in the air.

"What the f—" Susan started. "Susan!" Lori hissed, cutting her off.

Susan gave her a look, but Lori didn't flinch. She turned back to the being. "Uh, hi, Ahna. I'm Lori. This is Kamira. And Susan."

Kamira nodded, a little unsure about what was happening, but also curious. If Joseph Smith could have a visitation in the woods, why couldn't they? She also felt strangely safe, as if Ahna was exuding some sense of peace.

"We didn't say a prayer," Susan said, pulling Kamira towards her. "We don't even know if this thing is good or evil." She tugged at Lori's arm and whispered, "Didn't your parents ever give you the stranger danger talk?"

Lori gave Ahna a nervous glance. The being remained serene, waiting.

"You're right," Lori said softly. "We don't know what we're dealing with... yet." She turned to Kamira. "What do we do?"

"Wait, I've got this," Susan said, stepping forward. She gave Ahna a stern look and said, "Did Jesus Christ come in the flesh?"

Ahna grinned as she answered, "Yes."

Susan nodded and exhaled in relief.

"We're good, then," she said.

"How did you know to ask that?" Kamira asked.

"It's in the Bible," Susan frowned at their blank stares. "1 John 4? 'Every spirit that confesses that Jesus Christ has come in the flesh is from God.' Why are you two looking at me so weird? There is a literal spiritual or extraterrestrial being in the room with us!"

"Right," Lori said, placing her focus back on Ahna.

"Why are you here?"

"You made a request," Ahna said.

"But… we didn't pray. Not really," Lori said.

"It was in your hearts," Ahna smiled, looking at Lori, then Kamira and Susan. "That was enough."

"Give us a moment," Lori said and turned to consult with her friends. "What were we requesting, exactly?"

"Uh…," Kamira struggled to remember. "We felt like tonight was a wake-up call for something, but we weren't sure what we were supposed to get from it. And where do we draw the lines for trusting and not trusting people? Something like that, right?"

"Right. It wasn't fair to be punished for doing something nice," Lori added.

"We should have requested some food," Susan mumbled as her stomach gurgled. "Although I suppose we have that already." Susan reached into their snack stash and grabbed a chocolate-peanut-butter snack cake.

"Susan, can that wait?" Lori asked.

"You want one?" Susan asked Ahna. "I can't focus without something to eat."

"I do not require food, but please enjoy yours," Ahna said. "Nourishment matters."

Susan shrugged and kept chewing. "Preach."

Kamira and Lori followed suit. The sight of the cakes reminded them that they were pretty much starving.

"If you don't mind me asking," Lori said, "what are you?"

"I am Ahna," Ahna said once more.

"Do you have a spaceship?" Susan asked as she opened up a bag of BBQ chips.

"I do not require one," Ahna said.

"She materialized," Lori reminded her. "Obviously."

"Could've been beamed in," Susan muttered.

"I shifted into your density temporarily. I can see there has been a catalyst for expansion, but it is unclear what will develop from that. It's all dependent on your choices. How you use your free will. Your request for guidance, even in thought, allowed me to appear."

"Do you have guidance for us?" Kamira asked.

Ahna smiled.

"Just that the message of the evening was good even if its delivery was not," Ahna said. "Your choices are important. Seek God and follow His will. Also, support one another, and you will continue to grow and expand into fulfilled lives."

"My pants are going to expand if I keep eating these snacks, but they are so good," Susan said as she passed the chips on to Kamira and began opening a bag of chocolate candies.

"Sorry," she added after getting an annoyed look from Lori.

Ahna bowed her head.

"Are you leaving?" Lori asked, her tone a bit sad.

"I must move on. As do you."

Susan opened her mouth to ask something, but in a blink — Ahna vanished. The glow, the calm, the warmth — gone.

Kamira noticed right away that the heaviness of the night came flooding back. Her distrust of Jeri. The injustice of being tricked. Kamira became aware of the wood plank beneath her knees. Her mosquito bites itched.

"I was just getting ready to ask her something!" Susan pouted.

"That's probably why she left," Lori said with a coy smile.

Susan rolled her eyes, but she was smiling, too.

"Should we tell anyone?" Kamira asked.

"I don't think they'd believe us," Lori said.
"Maybe Christine would," Kamira offered with a sheepish grin.

Lori hesitated. "So, Ahna said — that this is an important moment. But... I don't know what that means. I don't feel any clearer."

"I don't know," Kamira said, then added, "Ahna said it was our choice. I felt better when I was back with both of you. Nothing really changed except I knew I wasn't alone anymore. And you helped me see things a little differently."

"How do you feel now?" Lori asked.

Kamira thought for a second.

"If I think about what happened with the kingdoms and Jeri, I get annoyed. But I also don't have to think about it. Being annoyed doesn't change anything except make me feel like I'm right and Jeri and the counselors are wrong."

Lori gave a slow nod.

"Yeah. Thinking about it as if we were wronged doesn't feel good. But maybe that's what shifted things — we got upset, we questioned everything, and somehow... that brought Ahna."

Susan tilted her head. "For real, though. Do you think Ahna was, like, an alien? Or an angel? Or an alien angel? Think she'll come back?"

Kamira shook her head. "No. That felt like a one-time thing. But it's weird how calm we are about it, right?"

Lori shrugged. "Isn't our church founded on a similar encounter? Don't we believe the afterlife is made up of planets? Honestly?

Christine might be more in tune than we thought."

Susan raised an eyebrow. "Okay, who are you and what have you done with Lori?"

"Shut up," Lori said, nudging her. "I can think outside the box."

Kamira chuckled. "Really, though, are we actually going to tell anyone what happened?"

"I don't know," Susan said. "Feels private."
"Yeah," Lori agreed. "Sacred or something."

Kamira looked thoughtful. "Is it weird that I'm already forgetting what Ahna looked like?"

Susan frowned. "She had feathers, right?"
"Feathers and a dress?" Lori offered, scrunching her face.

"That's not helpful," Susan said. "So... like Big Bird?"

They all laughed.

"Where's my journal?" Kamira said suddenly, hopping off her cot. She rummaged in a duffel bag and pulled it out. "I need to write this down before it fades completely."

"I'm so tired," Susan groaned, flopping into her sleeping bag.

"Same," Lori yawned, crawling into hers.

"We'll talk more in the morning," Susan mumbled. "After snacks."

"You never wake up early," Lori said. "Hmph," Susan grunted. "We'll see. I may be motivated to wake up for snacks."

As her friends drifted off, Kamira curled up with her notebook and pen. She scribbled as much as she could — Ahna's words, the way it felt, the way she'd felt.

Her handwriting slowed, then stopped. The pen slipped from her fingers as she fell asleep.

Onward

A trumpet blast jolted Kamira awake.

She blinked in the morning light and turned to see Lori already rolling up her sleeping bag, hair pulled back in a ponytail, clothes folded, eyes bright. Typical.

Across the cabin, Susan groaned and pulled her pillow over her head.

"Time to get up," Lori said. "There might still be warm water at the shower house if you hurry."

Kamira sat up slowly. "Wow. I slept hard."

"Me too," Lori said, stuffing her sleeping bag into its pouch. "Susan's still hibernating, though."

Lori picked up her pillow and lobbed it at Susan's cot. It landed with a satisfying *thud*.

Susan peeked out from under the pillow, groggy. "What is that thing made of? Bricks?"

"It's good for my neck," Lori replied. "And it's the last morning. We should try being on time for breakfast at least once."

Susan groaned but sat up, hair sticking out in every direction. "Fine, I'm up. I had the weirdest dream last night. We were talking to some kind of bird person."

"No way," Lori said. "I had a dream like that too."

Kamira froze. Something stirred in her memory. She reached for the journal on the floor next to her cot. On the front page was a sketch — a person-like creature in a flowy dress with feathers coming out its head. She'd written a few words beneath it:

"You have access to all the answers. Experience will uncover them. Support one another."

Kamira stared at the image. "Was it something like this?"

Susan leaned in. "That's it. That's the bird person. It *had* to be a dream... right?"

"We all dreamed the same thing?" Lori asked, then reflected. "I remember... we were about to pray, and then that... being appeared."

Kamira's brow furrowed. "How could we forget something like that?"

"Maybe our brains short-circuited," Susan muttered. "I'm not sure mine is processing it right now."

"What do we do?" Lori asked quietly.

Kamira shrugged. "What *can* we do?"

No answers came.

"I'm keeping this," Kamira said, hugging her journal. "If we ever forget, we'll remind each other."

"Does this mean we're going to alien cons to share our experience?" Susan asked with a grin.

"I'm not dressing up," Lori said.

Kamira laughed. "You two are the weirdest — and best — people I know. I'm glad to have you in my life."

"Whatever," Susan said, smirking. "I want some bacon in my life. Let's go."

They rushed to the shower house, then back to the cabin to pack their things. Kamira felt a lingering calm — like something had shifted inside. The sting of the previous night had dulled. There was no point wasting energy on people who wouldn't be part of her story beyond today.

She looked at her friends. The experience with Ahna, though vague and weird, had made the impression that the camp had intended to make with their theatrics, but had failed. Choosing well was something Kamira would now be contemplating for a while.

They made their way to breakfast. The mess hall buzzed with chatter. Kamira noticed how extra alert the girls were, scanning for elbows on tables. The tradition — embarrassing anyone who slipped up — was still going strong.

Sure enough, someone called out Paige — the quiet girl who'd managed to avoid attention all week. Kamira watched Paige rise slowly, pale and trembling.

"Sing something!" a voice shouted.

Paige's hands shook as she began a Primary song, voice barely above a whisper.

Susan looked at Kamira and Lori, rolled her eyes... and stood.

Paige faltered. The mess hall hushed.

"You don't have to do this," Susan said, walking to her side.

"Let her finish!" someone barked.

Susan turned to face the room.

"This is stupid," she said. "Why are we doing this? Who thought it was a good idea?"

"It's just a tradition," someone offered weakly.

Susan's voice rose. "Yeah, and maybe it's fun for you. But does *she* look like she's having fun?"

"It's good practice to step outside your comfort zone," another girl said.

"Who said that?" Susan scanned the room. "This isn't about confidence. It's about putting someone on the spot so you can laugh."

She paused, then leaned in over the table to stare down all the girls in the mess hall as she emphasized her next words:

"It is not heavenly."

The mess hall was silent as Susan finished speaking. She stood upright again, turned and motioned for Paige to sit down. Paige did.

Kamira saw girls exchanging wide-eyed glances. A few mouthed "geez" and "wow." Then, with theatrical flair, Susan sat back down and slammed both elbows on the table.

Kamira and Lori immediately followed suit.

No one called them out.

Paige smiled at Susan — a soft, grateful smile.

Sister Barbara stomped over and motioned for Susan to follow her out.

Lori and Kamira looked at one another and followed.

"I appreciate you were sticking up for Paige," Sister Barbara said as they stepped into the sunlight. "But these traditions were meant to be fun."

"Got it," Susan said. "Sorry. I'm not my usual self today. It's like a part of me died last night."

She smirked at Lori and Kamira. Lori stifled a laugh.

Sister Barbara hesitated, then sighed. "Just get your bags packed. Vans leave soon."

"Will do," Susan said cheerfully. "We're free to go?"

Sister Barbara nodded, already turning away.

"That was awesome," Lori said as they walked back to the cabin.

Kamira smiled. "You're like a superhero for the downtrodden."

"I like that better than the girl with the behavior problem and sassy mouth."

The three made it to their cabin, grabbed their things, and headed to the vans. Sister Sandra waved them over to their assigned one.

As they were stuffing their sleeping bags and backpacks in, Susan nudged Kamira and pointed out Jeri talking and laughing with her friends.

"Still think she's up to no good?" Susan said.

"I don't know," Kamira said slowly. "Maybe things aren't always that simple."

Lori joined them. "What are we looking at?"

In the distance, someone called Jeri's name. As she turned and walked towards the sound, she stumbled over some tree roots and almost fell, but caught herself in time.

Susan snorted.

"Guess she was moved by the spirit."

Lori elbowed Susan, but laughed. Kamira joined in as well.

"Time to go," Sister Sandra said, closing the back of the van.

Susan, Kamira, and Lori piled into the van with six other girls. Thankfully the air conditioner was on. Kamira realized that she hadn't heard or seen a mosquito since last night. It was a welcome absence.

Ahna
Illustration by Sheila Lee Brown

About Sheila Lee Brown

Sheila Lee Brown is a writer, artist, and generally very curious person. She spent her childhood playing outdoors in the woods surrounding her home and making up stories with her three siblings.

Sheila lives with her husband and their dog and enjoys writing, reading, drawing silly cartoons, and always learning and growing.

You can find out more about her upcoming projects at:

www.sheilaleebrown.com

Note from the Author

Thank you for reading my book! Writing this story was a fun, cathartic exercise as it was based on a similar experience I had at church camp (sans Ahna, of course!). I hope it was fun for you as well.

If you enjoyed reading this book, would you please take a moment to leave me a review at your favorite retailer?

Thanks, and best wishes!
Sheila Lee Brown